OTHER YEARLING BOOKS YOU WILL ENJOY:

YEARLING BOOKS/YOUNG YEARLINGS/YEARLING CLASSICS are designed especially to entertain and enlighten young people. Patricia Reilly Giff, consultant to this series, received the bachelor's degree from Marymount College. She holds the master's degree in history from St. John's University, and a Professional Diploma in Reading from Hofstra University. She was a teacher and reading consultant for many years, and is the author of numerous books for young readers.

For a complete listing of all Yearling titles, write to
Dell Readers Service, P.O. Box 1045,
South Holland, IL 60473.

Nate the Great
and the
STICKY CASE

Marjorie Weinman Sharmat

illustrations by Marc Simont

A YEARLING BOOK

Published by
Dell Publishing
a division of
The Bantam Doubleday Dell Publishing Group, Inc.
666 Fifth Avenue
New York, New York 10103

To my sister Rosalind,
who let me name Rosamond after her.

ISBN: 0-440-46289-4

Reprinted by arrangement with
Coward, McCann & Geoghegan, Inc.

Printed in the United States of America

June 1981

10 9

CW

To my sister Rosalind,
who let me name
Rosamond after her.

I, Nate the Great,
was drying off
from the rain.
I was sitting
under a blanket
and reading a detective book.
My dog Sludge was sniffing it.

I was on Page 33
when I heard a knock.
I opened the door.
Claude was there.
"I lost my best dinosaur,"
Claude said.
He was always losing things.
"This is your biggest loss yet,"
I said. "A dinosaur is huge.
How could you lose it?"
"My dinosaur is small,"
Claude said.
"It is a stegosaurus on a stamp.
Can you help me find it?"
"It is hard to find
something that small," I said.

"This will be a big case.
But I will take it.
Tell me, where was
the stegosaurus stamp
the last time you saw it?"

9

"It was on a table
in my house," Claude said.
"I was showing
all my dinosaur stamps
to my friends.
The stegosaurus stamp
was my favorite."
"Who are your friends?" I asked.
"Annie, Pip, Rosamond, and you.
But you weren't there,"
Claude added.

"Good thinking," I said.
"I, Nate the Great,
will go to your house
and look at your table."
I wrote a note to my mother.

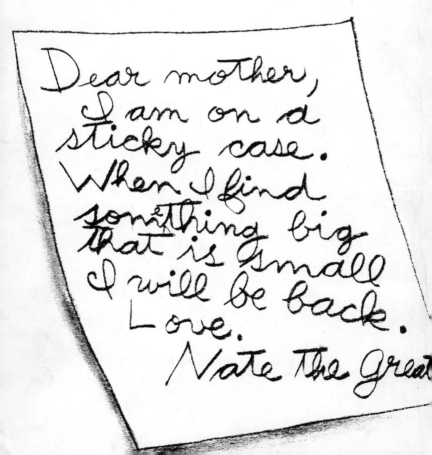

Claude and I went to his house.

He did not lose his way.

He showed me his table.

It had stamps all over it.

"Here are all of my stamps,"

Claude said. "Except for

the stegosaurus stamp."

I, Nate the Great,

saw a tyrannosaurus stamp.

I saw a brontosaurus stamp.

I saw an ichthyosaurus stamp.

I saw claws and jaws.

The stamps were ugly.

But that did not matter.

I had a case to solve.

I had a job to do.

"Where was the stegosaurus stamp
when it was on the table?"
I asked.
"Near the edge," Claude said.

14

STEGOSAURUS

"It must have fallen off,"
I said.
I looked on the floor
near the table.

The stegosaurus stamp
was not there.
I picked up a stamp
and showed it to Sludge.
"We must look for
a lost stamp," I said.
Sometimes Sludge is not
a great detective.
He tried to lick
the sticky side of the stamp.

"*Look*. Don't lick," I said.

Sludge and I looked at, over,

under, and around everything

in Claude's house.

Then we looked again.

We did not find

the stegosaurus stamp.

I, Nate the Great,
turned to Claude.
"The stegosaurus stamp
is not in your house," I said.
"Tell me, when did you notice
the stamp was missing?"
"After everybody left," Claude said.
"Did everybody leave together?"
I asked.
"Yes," said Claude.
"Did everybody come together?"
I asked.
"No," said Claude.
"Annie and Rosamond came
to tell me that Rosamond
was going to have a yard sale.

Then it started to rain.

It rained for a long time.

So Annie and Rosamond stayed

and looked at my stamps.

When the rain stopped,

Pip came over.

He looked at my stamps, too.

Then they all left together

to go to Rosamond's yard sale."

"Then I, Nate the Great,

must go to the yard sale, too,"

I said.

"I must speak to everyone

who was in the room

with the stegosaurus stamp."

Sludge and I

went to Rosamond's house.

Rosamond was standing

in her yard

with her four cats under a sign:

"Are you selling your cats?" I asked.

"No," Rosamond said.

"I am selling and swapping

empty tuna fish cans,

slippers, spare cat hairs,

toothbrushes, pictures of milk,

spoons, and all sorts of things."

Sludge was sniffing.

"Do you have

a stegosaurus stamp?" I asked.

"No," Rosamond said.

"But I saw one at Claude's house,

near the edge of his table."

"Thank you," I said.

I started to leave.

"Please buy a cat hair

from my yard sale,"

Rosamond called. "They are only
a penny each."
I, Nate the Great, did not want
a cat hair.
But I gave Rosamond a penny.
"I will buy one cat hair,"
I said.
"I will give you
an extra one free,"

Rosamond said.

"Do you want hairs
from Big Hex, Little Hex,
Plain Hex, or Super Hex?"

"Surprise me," I said.

Rosamond took a hair from a box
that was marked "Big Hex"
and a hair from a box
that was marked "Super Hex."

She stuck the hairs
to a piece of tape.

"So you won't lose them,"
she said.

Sometimes Rosamond
has strange ideas.

This was one of them.

I saw Pip looking at
some empty tuna fish cans.
"Did you see a stegosaurus stamp
at the edge of Claude's table?"
I asked.
Pip doesn't say much.

He shook his head
up and down.
"Do you know where it is now?"
I asked.
Pip shook his head
sideways.
"Thank you," I said.
I saw Annie and her dog Fang.
"I am looking for Claude's
stegosaurus stamp," I said.
"What do you know about it?"
"I know that the stegosaurus
is pretty," Annie said.
"I know that it looks like Fang."
Annie turned toward Fang.
"Show us your stegosaurus smile,"

she said.

Fang opened his mouth.

I, Nate the Great,

knew it was time

to go home.

I said good-by to Annie.

Sludge and I walked home slowly.

It was a good walk.

There were raindrops

on the tree leaves.

We saw ourselves in puddles.

We sniffed the clean air.

We saw a rainbow.

At home I made some pancakes.

I gave Sludge a bone.

We ate and thought.

Where was the stegosaurus stamp?

Nobody knew.

But the stamp was gone.

This was a sticky case.

I, Nate the Great, was stuck.

Then I thought,
perhaps there is
something different
about a stegosaurus stamp.
Perhaps I should think
about the stegosaurus
instead of the stamp.
Suddenly I, Nate, felt great.
I had pancakes in my stomach
and a good idea in my head.

STEGOSAURUS
Giant Lizard

"Wait here, Sludge," I said.

"I have to go look

for information."

I went to the museum.

I saw a stegosaurus there.

I had to look up.

And up. And up.

The stegosaurus was big.

He was bigger than Fang.

His smile was uglier.

But he could not move.

He could not do anything.

I, Nate the Great,

was glad about that.

I learned about the stegosaurus.

He was a giant lizard.

He lived a long time ago.

He had two brains.

I, Nate the Great, wished

that I had two brains

and that one of them

would solve this case.

I walked home.

The signs of rain were gone

except for some puddles.

I thought hard.

What did I know

about the stegosaurus stamp?

I knew that Annie and Rosamond

went to Claude's house

and saw the stamp.

Then it rained for a long time.

I knew that
after the rain stopped,
Pip went to Claude's house
and saw the stamp, too.
I knew the stamp had been
at the edge of Claude's table.
I knew it was not
in Claude's house now.

How did it get out
and where was it?
Seeing the big stegosaurus
had not helped the case.
Perhaps I had been thinking wrong.
Perhaps I had forgotten
that there are two sides
to every stamp.
Perhaps I should think about
the sticky side
instead of the stegosaurus side.
"Think sticky," I said
when I walked inside
and saw Sludge.
Sludge was licking his dog bowl.

He had not been much help
on this case.
Or had he?
I remembered when
Sludge tried to lick
the sticky side of a stamp.
Sludge's wet tongue
would have made the stamp
very sticky.

A very sticky stamp . . . sticks!
Suddenly I knew that
Sludge was a great detective.
He knew that the sticky side
of the stamp
could be important.
I, Nate the Great, knew
that anything wet
would make a stamp
very sticky.
I thought of wet things.
I thought of drips and drops.
I thought of rain.
When Annie and Rosamond
went to Claude's house
it was not raining.

But when Pip went
to Claude's house
it had been raining
and stopped.
Raindrops were on the trees.
Puddles were on the sidewalk.
Hmm.
I, Nate the Great,
thought of puddles.
I thought of Pip
stepping in them.
I got a stamp from my desk
and put it on the floor.
I went outside
and stepped in a few puddles.
Then I went back inside

and stepped on the sticky side
of the stamp.
The stamp stuck to my shoe!
The same thing
must have happened
to the stegosaurus stamp
and Pip's shoe
at Claude's house.
Sludge had given me
the clue I needed.
Now I knew
that I had to see Pip's shoes.

We went to Pip's house.

I rang the bell.

Pip opened the door.

I looked down at his feet.

He was wearing slippers.

"Where are your shoes?" I asked.

Pip looked down at his feet.

He opened his mouth.

Then he said,

"My shoes were all wet

from the rain.

After I left Claude's house

I swapped them

for a pair of dry slippers

at Rosamond's yard sale.

I took the slippers

off the Swap Table
and put my shoes there."
"Thank you," I said.
Sludge and I went back
to Rosamond's yard sale.
We went up to the Swap Table.
"The sticky case
is almost over," I said.

But Pip's shoes were not there.
Rosamond came over.
"I hope you don't want to swap
your cat hairs," she said.
"I want Pip's shoes," I said.
"Where are they?"
"I just sold them to Annie
for ten cents," Rosamond said.
"It was my big sale of the day."

Sludge and I ran to Annie's house.

She was outside with Fang.

I saw two shoes.

One was on the ground.

The other was in Fang's mouth.

"Are these Pip's shoes?" I asked.

"They were," Annie said.

"I bought them
for Fang to chew."
I, Nate the Great,
saw the bottom of the shoe
Fang was chewing.
Something small, square, and dirty
was stuck to it.

At last I had found
the stegosaurus stamp.
But I, Nate the Great, knew
that finding was not everything.
Getting was important, too.
I thought fast.
"Show me Fang's
stegosaurus smile," I said.
"Smile, Fang," Annie said.
Fang smiled.
The shoe fell to the ground.

I picked it up.
I, Nate the Great,
peeled off the stamp.
The case was solved.
We took the stegosaurus stamp
to Claude's house.
The stamp was dirty, sticky,
icky, and ugly.
But Claude was happy to get it.

Sludge and I walked home.
We were careful
not to step
in any puddles.